THE
ELEPHANT
AT THE
WALDORF

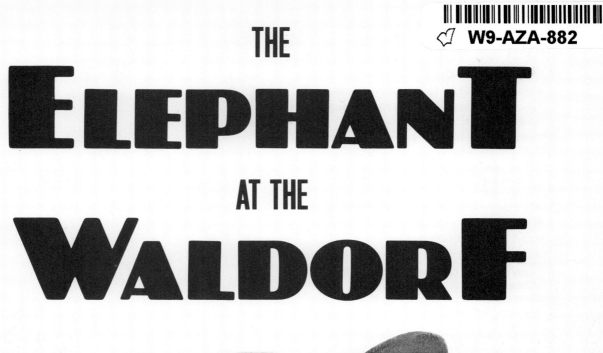

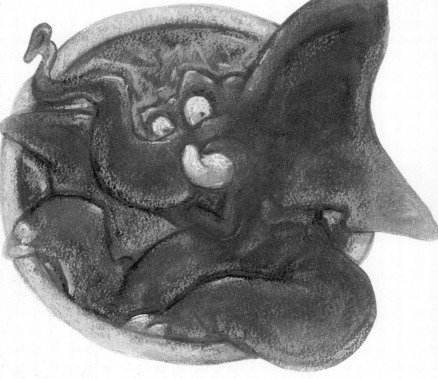

ANNE MIRANDA • DON VANDERBEEK

Troll Medallion

Published by Troll Medallion, an imprint and trademark of Troll Communications L.L.C.

First published in hardcover by BridgeWater Books.

Printed in the United States of America.

10 9 8 7 6 5 4 3 2 1

Library of Congress Cataloging-in-Publication Data
Miranda, Anne.
The elephant at The Waldorf / by Anne Miranda;
pictures by Don Vanderbeek.
p.   cm.
Summary: Members of a circus have trouble unloading a reluctant elephant from one of their trucks.
ISBN 0-8167-3452-6 (lib.)   ISBN 0-8167-3453-4 (pbk.)
[1. Elephants—Fiction.   2. Circus—Fiction.   3. Stories in rhyme.]   I. Vanderbeek, Don, ill.   II. Title.
PZ8.3.M657El   1995   [E]—dc20   93-33804

To Evan, Tyler, Kate and Paul,
and to my sisters Holly and Paula
for their love and support.

A.M.

In memory of
Carrie Anne Vanderbeek:
"A star is mighty fine company."

D.V.

At The Waldorf Astoria, one summer night,
my mother and I saw a startling sight.
Circus trucks pulled up and parked in a line,
ignoring the noise and the NO PARKING sign.

A driver jumped out from his truck to the block.
He took out a key and unlocked a big lock.

He lowered a ramp and then, to our amazement,
tried coaxing an *elephant* onto the pavement.

A circus girl climbed on the elephant's back.
The man snapped a whip with a crickety-crack.

They offered her boxes of popcorn to eat.
But the elephant wouldn't step onto the street.

A spangled trapeze artist tickled her nose.
A circus magician pulled out a rose.

My mother and I gave her peanuts to try.
She turned up her trunk with a sniff and a sigh.

Acrobats tumbled and begged her to leave.
A dwarf pulled an elephant doll from his sleeve.
The ringmaster called out the elephant's name.
The fire-eater lit up and swallowed a flame.

An upside-down clown turned around on one hand.
The orchestra leader conducted the band,

as a fat lady warbled her favorite ditty.
The elephant sat there and watched New York City.

The near-frantic head of The Waldorf hotel
looked at the clock. Then he said with a yell,
"The curtain goes up fifteen minutes from now!
That elephant has to get in here somehow."

We stood and we wondered what more could be done,
when, finally, the trainer arrived with his son.
He twirled off his cape with a whirl of his hands,
and bowed very deeply to greet all his fans.

"Stand back everybody. Now *I* am in charge!
I can move any elephant, tiny or large."
He tugged and he pulled. Then he ordered and shouted.
He made funny faces. He cried and he pouted.

He tried everything he could think of to do.
He tried some old tricks and a few that were new.
But the trainer gave up with a minute to go.
He said he was sorry and canceled the show.

Then a young boy in a tux and a tie
said very quietly, "Dad, may I try?"

His father agreed and the boy took his turn.
He winked at the elephant. "When will they learn?"

He patted her sweetly. "Don't stay here all night.
PLEASE, won't you come?" He was very polite.

Like magic, from that dark and hay-covered floor,
the elephant stood up and squeezed through the door.
She raced down the ramp and then onto the street.
She wiggled her ears and reared up on two feet.

Then offering her trunk to the doorman named Bobby,
she walked up the steps and waltzed into the lobby.
The crowd on the sidewalk was swept with euphoria,
as the elephant entered The Waldorf Astoria!

The rest of the circus acts hurried inside.
The animal trainer applauded with pride.

His son saved the day with a second to spare.
He hugged him and kissed him and rumpled his hair.

The people who'd watched gave a standing ovation.
They yelled and they shouted with deep admiration.
The boy took a bow and they both disappeared.
My mother and I waved good-bye and we cheered.

We wished we could follow them in from the street.
The Waldorf Astorians were in for a treat.

Imagine the circus girls sparkling and prancing!
In some golden ballroom an elephant's dancing.

Then I got to thinking. I looked at my mother.
We had the same thought as we stared at each other.
We both started giggling and laughed 'til we cried.
How would that elephant get back outside?